WILD ACTION NEWS
FOCUS, FENNEC FOX!

by J.L. Anderson   illustrated by Amanda Erb

Rourke
Educational Media
rourkeeducationalmedia.com

A Division of
Carson Dellosa Education

Dear Guardian/Educator,
Introduce your child to the wonderful world of reading with our leveled
readers. Your growing reader will be continuously engaged as he or she
is guided from one level to the next. Each level is carefully built to provide
your child with the reading skills and knowledge to be a confident
reader! Ultimately, we want your child to develop a love of reading.

Level 1 *Learning to Read*
High frequency words, basic sentences, large type, labels, full color
illustrations to help young readers better comprehend the text

Level 2 *Beginning to Read Alone*
Short sentences, familiar words, simple plot, easy-to-read fonts

Level 3 *Reading on Your Own*
Short paragraphs, easy-to-follow plots, vocabulary is increasingly
challenging, exciting stories

Level 4 *Proficient Reader*
Chapters, engaging stories, challenging vocabulary, multiple text features

Reading should be a pleasurable experience. A child who enjoys reading
reads more, and a child who reads more becomes a better reader.
Your child will grow with exposure to broad vocabulary and literary
techniques, and will develop deeper critical thinking and comprehension
skills. We are excited to be a part of your child's reading journey.

Happy reading,
Rourke Educational Media

www.rourkeeducationalmedia.com

Edited by: Kim Thompson
Cover and interior layout by: Rhea Magaro-Wallace
Cover and interior illustrations by: Amanda Erb

Library of Congress PCN Data

Focus, Fennec Fox! / J.L. Anderson
(WILD Action News)
ISBN 978-1-73161-499-5 (hard cover)(alk. paper)
ISBN 978-1-73161-306-6 (soft cover)
ISBN 978-1-73161-604-3 (e-Book)
ISBN 978-1-73161-709-5 (ePub)
Library of Congress Control Number: 2019932406

Table of Contents

Chapter One
On Assignment

Fennec Fox with WILD Action News here! I'm on **assignment** in the desert.

I am on scene at the camel beauty pageant. I wanted to cover the camel races. That's always a big story! But Kangaroo Rat got picked to cover that.

"You must prove you can stay focused," my **producer** said. "Find a good story at the pageant. Something **newsworthy** is bound to happen there."

A good news report answers these questions: *Who? What? When? Where? Why? How?*

There is a lot going on at the pageant. I'm not sure what to focus on. Should I report on the camels' costumes? Or their dance routines?

I need to get some information about camels. And beauty pageants! That will help me decide what is newsworthy about this event.

My huge ears help me
gather information. I have the
largest ears of any dog or fox.
My ears hear an ant nearby.
Chomp!

Insects are a tasty treat.

Did you know there are

desert insects called camel

spiders? They can be as long

as my ears.

Oops, I'm losing focus.

I'm not here to report about

insects. I have to stay on task.

Chapter Two
What's the Story?

I spot a group of camels. I can interview them for information. I need to ask questions!

Reporters ask questions to gather facts. They share the facts with others. Reporters keep everyone informed!

I get my camera ready.

"Fennec Fox with WILD Action News here," I say. "May I ask you some questions?"

"Yes," the camels say. One camel spits. I think that means "No."

"What makes a camel beautiful?" I ask.

"The hump on my back is beautiful," a camel says. "Did you know it is made of fat, not water?"

"My large, lovely feet
help me walk on the sand,"
another camel says.

The camels start talking all

at once.

"My thick lips help me eat

thorny plants."

"My long eyelashes are pretty. They protect me from the blowing sand."

The camels go on and on. I can't keep up!

Luckily, my camera is recording everything. But I still need to take careful notes.

I also need more than a list of facts for this story.

I need some background. I need some **B-roll** too! I film some shots of the crowd. I will show this footage while I give my news report later.

MY REPORT! I still don't

have a story!

I walk around. I see a sign. It says, "Camels are a symbol of desert life. Did you know camels can go months without food?"

I watch a camel drink
enough water to fill a fish
tank. It is SO hot and dry in
the desert! I'm glad my big fox
ears help me lose body heat.

Chapter Three

Some Bite!

The pageant will start soon.
Some camel contestants
walk by me. I hear some
whispering. I can't make out
the words.

A few camels kneel down in the soft sand to rest.

I yawn. The heat is making me sleepy.

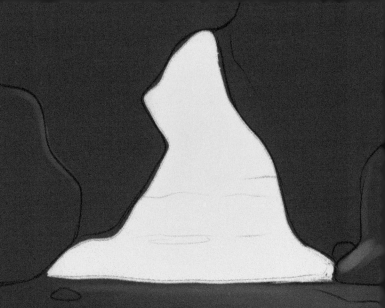

I usually sleep during the day. I hunt for food at night. That is how foxes stay cool during the hottest part of the day.

I need to find my **angle** for
this story. I also need a break.
I find a den and cool off.

I am dozing off when I hear

a camel say, "cheat."

I am focused now! I turn on
my camera. "Excuse me," I
say. "Did you say 'cheat'?"

"Yes," the camel says. "One of the contestants was caught eating the scorecards!"

"But the show must go on!" another camel says.

Cheating at the pageant. I
think I found my story. And
this story has some bite!

It's time to go live with the news! I interview the scorecard chewer. It's important to get all sides of a story.

"I was just hungry," he says.

Bonus Stuff!

Glossary

angle (ANG-guhl): The point or theme of a news article or feature story.

assignment (uh-SINE-muhnt): A job given to someone.

B-roll (bee-rohl): Extra footage taken to enrich a story.

newsworthy (NOOZ-wur-thee): Important or interesting enough for a news story.

producer (pruh-DOOS-er): The person in charge of managing a TV broadcast.

Discussion Questions

1. Think about what happened to you yesterday. Which event was most newsworthy?

2. When does Fennec Fox's story idea come to him? Why is it important for a reporter to always be alert?

3. In what ways does Fennec Fox gather information about camels?

Activity: Camel Print

Use your handprint to craft a creative camel!

Supplies

- brown washable paint
- paper plate
- paintbrush
- construction paper
- black marker

Directions

1. Pour a small amount of brown paint on the paper plate. Use the paintbrush to coat your hand with a thin layer of paint.

2. Make a handprint by pressing your painted hand on the construction paper with fingers spread wide. Wash your hand.

3. Turn the print upside down so the four fingers point down. These will be the camel's legs.

4. Paint a hump and a tail on the camel. At the tip of the thumbprint, paint a curved line upward to make the camel's neck. Add a head. Let the paint dry.

5. Use the black marker to add hooves, an eye, a mouth, an ear, or other details to your camel's profile. Host your own camel beauty pageant with your friends by hanging up your creations!

Writing Prompt

Imagine you are a fennic fox with huge ears that can hear everything! Listen carefully when you are outside, at school, or in a crowded place. Research and write an article about the most newsworthy thing you hear.

About the Author

J.L. Anderson is always curious to get the scoop! She loves writing for kids of all ages, and she's passionate about animals and nature. You can learn more about her by visiting www.jessicaleeanderson.com.

About the Illustrator

Amanda is always on the lookout for new stories to illustrate! Some of her favorite stories to illustrate involve expressive animal and human characters. You can find more of her work at www.amandaerb.com.